Rudyard Kipling's Bridge Builders

Index Of Contents

The Bridge Builders
Rudyard Kipling – A Biography

The least that Findlayson, of the Public Works Department, expected was a C.I.E.; he dreamed of a C.S.I. Indeed, his friends told him that he deserved more. For three years he had endured heat and cold, disappointment, discomfort, danger, and disease, with responsibility almost to top-heavy for one pair of shoulders; and day by day, through that time, the great Kashi Bridge over the Ganges had grown under his charge. Now, in less than three months, if all went well, his Excellency the Viceroy would open the bridge in state, an archbishop would bless it, and the first trainload of soldiers would come over it, and there would be speeches.

Findlayson, C. E., sat in his trolley on a construction line that ran along one of the main revetments - the huge stone-faced banks that flared away north and south for three miles on either side of the river and permitted himself to think of the end. With its approaches, his work was one mile and three-quarters in length; a lattice-girder bridge, trussed with the Findlayson truss standing on seven-and-twenty brick piers. Each one of those piers was twenty-four feet in diameter, capped with red Agra stone and sunk eighty feet below the shifting sand of the Ganges' bed. Above them was a railway-line fifteen feet broad; above that, again, a cart-road of eighteen feet, flanked with footpaths. At either end rose towers, of red brick, loopholed for musketry and pierced for big guns, and the ramp of the road was being pushed forward to their haunches. The raw earth-ends were crawling and alive with hundreds upon hundreds of tiny asses climbing out of the yawning borrow-pit below with sackfuls of stuff; and the hot afternoon air was filled with the noise of hooves, the rattle of the drivers' sticks, and the swish and roll-down of the dirt. The river was very low, and on the dazzling white sand between the three centre piers stood squat cribs of railway-sleepers, filled within and daubed without with mud, to support the last of the girders as those were riveted up. In the little deep water left by the drought, an overhead crane travelled to and fro along its spile-pier, jerking sections of iron into place, snorting and backing and grunting as an elephant grunts in the timberyard. Riveters by the hundred swarmed about the lattice side-work and the iron roof of the railway line hung from invisible staging under the bellies of the girders, clustered round the throats of the piers, and rode on the overhang of the footpath-stanchions; their fire-pots and the spurts of flame that answered each hammer-stroke showing no more than pale yellow in the sun's glare. East and west and north and south the construction-trains rattled and shrieked up and down the embankments, the piled trucks of brown and white stone banging behind them till the side-boards were unpinned, and with a roar and a grumble a few thousand tons' more material were flung out to hold the river in place.

Findlayson, C. E., turned on his trolley and looked over the face of the country that he had changed for seven miles around. Looked back on the humming village of five thousand work-men; up stream and down, along the vista of spurs and sand; across the river to the far piers, lessening in the haze; overhead to the guard-towers -and only he knew how strong those were - and with a sigh of contentment saw that his work was good. There stood his bridge before him in the sunlight, lacking only a few weeks' work on the girders of the three middle piers - his bridge, raw and ugly as original sin, but pukka - permanent - to endure when all memory of the builder, yea, even of the splendid Findlayson truss, has perished. Practically, the thing was done.

Hitchcock, his assistant, cantered along the line on a little switch-tailed Kabuli pony who through long practice could have trotted securely over trestle, and nodded to his chief.

"All but," said he, with a smile.

"I've been thinking about it," the senior answered. "Not half a bad job for two men, is it?"

"One - and a half. 'Gad, what a Cooper's Hill cub I was when I came on the works!" Hitchcock felt very old in the crowded experiences of the past three years, that had taught him power and responsibility.

"You were rather a colt," said Findlayson. "I wonder how you'll like going back to office-work when this job's over."

"I shall hate it!" said the young man, and as he went on his eye followed Findlayson's, and he muttered, "Isn't it damned good?"

"I think we'll go up the service together," Findlayson said to himself. "You're too good a youngster to waste on another man. Cub thou wast; assistant thou art. Personal assistant, and at Simla, thou shalt be, if any credit comes to me out of the business!"

Indeed, the burden of the work had fallen altogether on Findlayson and his assistant, the young man whom he had chosen because of his rawness to break to his own needs. There were labour contractors by the half-hundred - fitters and riveters, European, borrowed from the railway workshops, with, perhaps, twenty white and half-caste subordinates to direct, under direction, the bevies of workmen - but none knew better than these two, who trusted each other, how the underlings were not to be trusted. They had been tried many times in sudden crises - by slipping of booms, by breaking of tackle, failure of cranes, and the wrath of the river - but no stress had brought to light any man among men whom Findlayson and Hitchcock would have honoured by working as remorselessly as they worked them-selves. Findlayson thought it over from the beginning: the months of offce-work destroyed at a blow when the Government of India, at the last moment, added two feet to the width of the bridge, under the impression that bridges were cut out of paper, and so brought to ruin at least half an acre of calculations- and Hitchcock, new to disappointment, buried his head in his arms and wept; the heart-breaking delays over the filling of the contracts in England; the futile correspondences hinting at great wealth of commissions if one, only one, rather doubtful consignment were passed; the war that followed the refusal; the careful, polite obstruction at the other end that followed the war, till young Hitchcock, putting one month's leave to another month, and borrowing ten days from Findlayson, spent his poor little savings of a year in a wild dash to London, and there, as his own tongue asserted and the later consignments proved, put the fear of God into a man so great that he feared only Parliament and said so till Hitchcock wrought with him across his own dinner table, and - he feared the Kashi Bridge and all who spoke in its name. Then there was the cholera that came in the night to the village by the bridge works; and after the cholera smote the small-pox. The fever they had always with them. Hitchcock had been appointed a magistrate of the third class with whipping powers, for the better government of the community, and Findlayson watched him wield his powers temperately, learning what to overlook and what to look after. It was a long, long reverie, and it covered storm, sudden freshets, death in every manner and shape, violent and awful rage against red tape half frenzying a mind that knows it should be busy on other things; drought, sanitation, finance; birth, wedding, burial, and riot in the village of twenty warring castes; argument, expostulation, persuasion, and the blank despair that a man goes to bed upon, thankful that his rifle is all in pieces in the gun-case. Behind everything rose the black frame of the Kashi Bridge - plate by plate, girder by girder, span by span - and each pier of it recalled Hitchcock, the all-round man, who had stood by his chief without failing from the very first to this last.

So the bridge was two men's work - unless one counted Peroo, as Peroo certainly counted himself. He was a Lascar, a Kharva from Bulsar, familiar with every port between Rockhampton and London, who had risen to the rank of serang on the British India boats, but wearying of routine musters and clean clothes, had thrown up the service and gone inland, where men of his calibre were sure of employment. For his knowledge of tackle and the handling of heavy weights, Peroo was worth almost any price he might have chosen to put upon his services; but custom decreed the wage of the overhead-men, and Peroo was not within many silver pieces of his proper value. Neither running water nor extreme heights made him afraid; and, as an ex-serang, he knew how to hold authority. No piece of iron was so big or so badly placed that Peroo could not devise a tackle to lift it - a loose-ended, sagging arrangement, rigged with a scandalous amount of talking, but perfectly equal to the work in hand. It was Peroo who had saved the girder of Number Seven pier from destruction when the new wire-rope jammed in the eye of the crane, and the huge plate tilted in its slings, threatening to slide out sideways. Then the native workmen lost their heads with great shoutings, and Hitchcock's right arm was broken by a falling T-plate, and he buttoned it up in his coat and swooned, and came to and directed for four hours till Peroo, from the top of the crane, reported "All's well," and the plate swung home. There was no one like Peroo, serang, to lash, and guy, and hold, to control the donkey-engines, to hoist a fallen locomotive craftily out of the borrow-pit into which it had tumbled; to strip, and dive, if need be, to see how the concrete blocks round the piers stood the scouring of Mother Gunga, or to adventure upstream on a monsoon night and report on the state of the embankment-facings. He would interrupt the field-councils of Findlayson and Hitchcock without fear, till his wonderful English, or his still more wonderful linguafranca, half Portuguese and half Malay, ran out and he was forced to take string and show the knots that he would recommend. He controlled his own gang of tackle men - mysterious relatives from Kutch Mandvi gathered month by month and tried to the uttermost. No consideration of family or kin allowed Peroo to keep weak hands or a giddy head on the pay-roll. "My honour is the honour of this bridge," he would say to the about-to-be-dismissed. "What do I care for your honour? Go and work on a steamer. That is all you are fit for."

The little cluster of huts where he and his gang lived centred round the tattered dwelling of a sea-priest - one who had never set foot on black water, but had been chosen as ghostly counsellor by two generations of sea-rovers all unaffected by port missions or those creeds which are thrust upon sailors by agencies along Thames bank. The priest of the Lascars had nothing to do with their caste, or indeed with anything at all. He ate the offerings of his church, and slept and smoked, and slept again, "for," said Peroo, who had haled him a thousand miles inland, "he is a very holy man. He never cares what you eat so long as you do not eat beef, and that is good, because on land we worship Shiva, we Kharvas; but at sea on the Kumpani's boats we attend strictly to the orders of the Burra Malum [the first mate], and on this bridge we observe what Finlinson Sahib says."

Finlinson Sahib had that day given orders to clear the scaffolding from the guard-tower on the right bank, and Peroo with his mates was casting loose and lowering down the bamboo poles and planks as swiftly as ever they had whipped the cargo out of a coaster.

From his trolley he could hear the whistle of the serang's silver pipe and the creek and clatter of the pulleys. Peroo was standing on the top-most coping of the tower, clad in the blue dungaree of his abandoned service, and as Findlayson motioned to him to be careful, for his was no life to throw away, he gripped the last pole, and, shading his eyes ship-fashion, answered with the long-drawn wail of the fo'c'sle lookout: "Ham dekhta hai" ("I am looking out").

Findlayson laughed and then sighed. It was years since he had seen a steamer, and he was sick for home. As his trolley passed under the tower, Peroo descended by a rope, ape-fashion, and cried: "It looks well now, Sahib. Our bridge is all but done. What think you Mother Gunga will say when the rail runs over?"

"She has said little so far. It was never Mother Gunga that delayed us."

"There is always time for her; and none the less there has been delay. Has the Sahib forgotten last autumn's flood, when the stone-boats were sunk without warning - or only a half-day's warning?"

"Yes, but nothing save a big flood could hurt us now. The spurs are holding well on the West Bank."

"Mother Gunga eats great allowances. There is always room for more stone on the revetments. I tell this to the Chota Sahib" - he meant Hitchcock - "and he laughs."

"No matter, Peroo. Another year thou wilt be able to build a bridge in thine own fashion."

The Lascar grinned. "Then it will not be in this way - with stonework sunk under water, as the Qyetta was sunk. I like sus-sus-pen-sheen bridges that fly from bank to bank. with one big step, like a gang-plank. Then no water can hurt. When does the Lord Sahib come to open the bridge?"

"In three months, when the weather is cooler."

"Ho! ho! He is like the Burra Malum. He sleeps below while the work is being done. Then he comes upon the quarter-deck and touches with his finger, and says: 'This is not clean! Dam jibboonwallah!'"

"But the Lord Sahib does not call me a dam jibboonwallah, Peroo."

"No, Sahib; but he does not come on deck till the work is all finished. Even the Burra Malum of the Nerbudda said once at Tuticorin -"

"Bah! Go! I am busy."

"I, also!" said Peroo, with an unshaken countenance. "May I take the light dinghy now and row along the spurs?"

"To hold them with thy hands? They are, I think, sufficiently heavy."

"Nay, Sahib. It is thus. At sea, on the Black Water, we have room to be blown up and down without care. Here we have no room at all. Look you, we have put the river into a dock, and run her between stone sills."

Findlayson smiled at the "we."

"We have bitted and bridled her. She is not like the sea, that can beat against a soft beach. She is Mother Gunga - in irons." His voice fell a little.

"Peroo, thou hast been up and down the world more even than I. Speak true talk, now. How much dost thou in thy heart believe of Mother Gunga?"

"All that our priest says. London is London, Sahib. Sydney is Sydney, and Port Darwin is Port Darwin. Also Mother Gunga is Mother Gunga, and when I come back to her banks I know this and worship. In London I did poojah to the big temple by the river for the sake of the God within. . . . Yes, I will not take the cushions in the dinghy."

Findlayson mounted his horse and trotted to the shed of a bungalow that he shared with his assistant. The place had become home to him in the last three years. He had grilled in the heat, sweated in the rains, and shivered with fever under the rude thatch roof; the lime-wash beside the door was covered with rough drawings and formulae, and the sentry-path trodden in the matting of the verandah showed where he had walked alone. There is no eight-hour limit to an engineer's work, and the evening meal with Hitchcock was eaten booted and spurred: over their cigars they listened to the hum of the village as the gangs came up from the river-bed and the lights began to twinkle.

"Peroo has gone up the spurs in your dinghy. He's taken a couple of nephews with him, and he's lolling in the stern like a commodore," said Hitchcock.

"That's all right. He's got something on his mind. You'd think that ten years in the British India boats would have knocked most of his religion out of him."

"So it has," said Hitchcock, chuckling. "I overheard him the other day in the middle of a most atheistical talk with that fat old guru of theirs. Peroo denied the efficacy of prayer; and wanted the guru to go to sea and watch a gale out with him, and see if he could stop a monsoon."

"All the same, if you carried off his guru he'd leave us like a shot. He was yarning away to me about praying to the dome of St. Paul's when he was in London."

"He told me that the first time he went into the engine-room of a steamer, when he was a boy, he prayed to the low-pressure cylinder."

"Not half a bad thing to pray to, either. He's propitiating his own Gods now, and he wants to know what Mother Gunga will think of a bridge being run across her. Who's there?" A shadow darkened the doorway, and a telegram was put into Hitchcock's hand.

"She ought to be pretty well used to it by this time. Only a tar. It ought to be Ralli's answer about the new rivets. . . . Great Heavens!" Hitchcock jumped to his feet.

"What is it?" said the senior, and took the form. "that's what Mother Gunga thinks, is it," he said, reading. "Keep cool, young 'un. We've got all our work cut out for us. Let's see. Muir wired half an hour ago: 'Floods on the Ramgunga. Look out.' Well, that gives us - one, two - nine and a half for the flood to reach Melipur Ghaut and seven's sixteen and a half to Lataoli - say fifteen hours before it comes down to us."

"Curse that hill-fed sewer of a Ramgunga! Findlayson, this is two months before anything could have been expected, and the left bank is littered up with stuff still. Two full months before the time!"

"That's why it comes. I've only known Indian rivers for five-and-twenty years, and I don't pretend to understand. Here comes another tar." Findlayson opened the telegram. "Cockran, this time, from the Ganges Canal: 'Heavy rains here. Bad.' He might have saved the last word. Well, we don't want to know any more. We've got to work the gangs all night and clean up the riverbed. You'll take the east bank and work out to meet me in the middle. Get everything that floats below the bridge: we shall have quite enough river-craft coming down adrift anyhow, without letting the stone-boats ram the piers. What have you got on the east bank that needs looking after?

"Pontoon - one big pontoon with the overhead crane on it. T'other overhead crane on the mended pontoon, with the cart-road rivets from Twenty to Twenty-three piers - two construction lines, and a turning-spur. The pilework must take its chance," said Hitchcock.

"All right. Roll up everything you can lay hands on. We'll give the gang fifteen minutes more to eat their grub."

Close to the verandah stood a big night-gong, never used except for flood, or fire in the village. Hitchcock had called for a fresh horse, and was off to his side of the bridge when Findlayson took the cloth-bound stick and smote with the rubbing stroke that brings out the full thunder of the metal.

Long before the last rumble ceased every night-gong in the village had taken up the warning. To these were added the hoarse screaming of conches in the little temples; the throbbing of drums and tom-toms; and, from the European quarters, where the riveters lived, McCartney's bugle, a weapon of offence on Sundays and festivals, brayed desperately, calling to "Stables." Engine after engine toiling home along the spurs at the end of her day's work whistled in answer till the whistles were answered from the far bank. Then the big gong thundered thrice for a sign that it was flood and not fire; conch, drum, and whistle echoed the call, and the village quivered to the sound of bare feet running upon soft earth. The order in all cases was to stand by the day's work and wait instructions. The gangs poured by in the dusk; men stopping to knot a loin-cloth or fasten a sandal; gang-foremen shouting to their subordinates as they ran or paused by the tool-issue sheds for bars and mattocks; locomotives creeping down their tracks wheel-deep in the crowd; till the brown torrent disappeared into the dusk of the river-bed, raced over the pilework, swarmed along the lattices, clustered by the cranes, and stood still - each man in his place.

Then the troubled beating of the gong carried the order to take up everything and bear it beyond high-water mark, and the flare-lamps broke out by the hundred between the webs of dull iron as the riveters began a night's work, racing against the flood that was to come. The girders of the three centre piers - those that stood on the cribs -were all but in position. They needed just as many rivets as could be driven into them, for the flood would assuredly wash out their supports, and the ironwork would settle down on the caps of stone if they were not blocked at the ends. A hundred crowbars strained at the sleepers of the temporary line that fed the unfinished piers. It was heaved up in lengths, loaded into trucks, and backed up the bank beyond flood-level by the groaning locomotives. The tool-sheds on the sands melted away before the attack of shouting armies, and with them went the stacked ranks of Government stores, iron-hound boxes of rivets, pliers, cutters, duplicate parts of the riveting-machines, spare pumps and chains. The big crane would be the last to be shifted, for she was hoisting all the heavy stuff up to the main structure of the bridge. The concrete blocks on the fleet of stone-boats were dropped overside, where there was any depth of water, to guard the piers, and the empty boats themselves were poled under the bridge down-stream. It was here that Peroo's pipe shrilled loudest, for the first stroke of the big gong had brought the dinghy back at racing speed, and Peroo and his people were stripped to the waist, working for the honour and credit which are better than life.

"I knew she would speak," he cried. "I knew, but the telegraph gives us good warning. O sons of unthinkable begetting - children of unspeakable shame - are we here for the look of the thing?" It was two feet of wire-rope frayed at the ends, and it did wonders as Peroo leaped from gunnel to gunnel, shouting the language of the sea.

Findlayson was more troubled for the stoneboats than anything else. McCartney, with his gangs, was blocking up the ends of the three doubtful spans. but boats adrift, if the flood chanced to be a high one, might endanger the girders; and there was a very fleet in the shrunken channel.

"Get them behind the swell of the guardtower," he shouted down to Peroo. "It will be dead-water there. Get them below the bridge."

"Accha! [Very good.] I know; we are mooring them with wire-rope," was the answer. "Heh! Listen to the Chota Sahib. He is working hard."

From across the river came an almost continuous whistling of locomotives, backed by the rumble of stone. Hitchcock at the last minute was spending a few hundred more trucks of Tarakee stone in reinforcing his spurs and embankments.

"The bridge challenges Mother Gunga," said Peroo, with a laugh.

"But when she talks I know whose voice will be the loudest."

For hours the naked men worked, screaming and shouting under the lights. It was a hot, moonless night; the end of it was darkened by clouds and a sudden squall that made Findlayson very grave.

"She moves!" said Peroo, just before the dawn. "Mother Gunga is awake! Hear!" He dipped his hand over the side of a boat and the current mumbled on it. A little wave hit the side of a pier with a crisp slap.

"Six hours before her time," said Findlayson, mopping his forehead savagely.

"Now we can't depend on anything. We'd better clear all hands out of the riverbed."

Again the big gong beat, and a second time there was the rushing of naked feet on earth and ringing iron; the clatter of tools ceased. In the silence, men heard the dry yawn of water crawling over thirsty sand.

Foreman after foreman shouted to Findlayson, who had posted himself by the guard-tower, that his section of the river-bed had been cleaned out, and when the last voice dropped Findlayson hurried over the bridge till the iron plating of the permanent way gave place to the temporary plank-walk over the three centre piers, and there he met Hitchcock.

"'All clear your side?" said Findlayson. The whisper rang in the box of lattice work.

"Yes, and the east channel's filling now. We're utterly out of our reckoning. When is this thing down on us?"

"There's no saying. She's filling as fast as she can. Look!" Findlayson pointed to the planks below his feet, where the sand, burned and defiled by months of work, was beginning to whisper and fizz.

"What orders?" said Hitchcock.

"Call the roll - count stores sit on your hunkers - and pray for the bridge. That's all I can think of Good night. Don't risk your life trying to fish out anything that may go downstream."

"Oh, I'll be as prudent as you are! 'Night. Heavens, how she's filling! Here's the rain in earnest."

Findlayson picked his way back to his bank, sweeping the last of McCartney's riveters before him. The gangs had spread themselves along the embankments, regardless of the cold rain of the dawn, and there they waited for the flood. Only Peroo kept his men together behind the swell of the guard-tower, where the stone-boats lay tied fore and aft with hawsers, wire-rope, and chains.

A shrill wail ran along the line, growing to a yell, half fear and half wonder: the face of the river whitened from bank to hank between the stone facings, and the far-away spurs went out in spouts of foam. Mother Gunga had come bank-high in haste, and a wall of chocolate-coloured water was her messenger. There was a shriek above the roar of the water, the complaint of the spans coming down on their blocks as the cribs were whirled out from under their bellies. The stone-boats groaned and ground each other in the eddy that swung round the abutment, and their clumsy masts rose higher and higher against the dim sky-line.

"Before she was shut between these walls we knew what she would do. Now she is thus cramped God only knows what she will do!" said Peroo, watching the furious turmoil round the guard-tower. "Ohe'! Fight, then! Fight hard, for it is thus that a woman wears herself out."

But Mother Gunga would not fight as Peroo desired. After the first down-stream plunge there came no more walls of water, but the river lifted herself bodily, as a snake when she drinks in midsummer, plucking and fingering along the revetments, and banking up behind the piers till even Findlayson began to recalculate the strength of his work.

When day came the village gasped. "Only last night," men said, turning to each other, "it was as a town in the river-bed! Look now!"

And they looked and wondered afresh at the deep water, the racing water that licked the throat of the piers. The farther bank was veiled by rain, into which the bridge ran out and vanished; the spurs up-stream were marked by no more than eddies and spoutings, and down-stream the pent river, once freed of her guide-lines, had spread like a sea to the horizon. Then hurried by, rolling in the water, dead men and oxen together, with here and there a patch of thatched roof that melted when it touched a pier.

"Big flood," said Peroo, and Findlayson nodded. It was as big a flood as he had any wish to watch. His bridge would stand what was upon her now, but not very much more, and if by any of a thousand chances there happened to be a weakness in the embankments, Mother Gunga would carry his honour to the sea with the other raffle. Worst of all, there was nothing to do except to sit still; and Findlayson sat still under his macintosh till his helmet became pulp on his head, and his boots were over-ankle in mire. He took no count of time, for the river was marking the hours, inch by inch and foot by foot, along the embankment, and he listened, numb and hungry, to the straining of the stone-boats, the hollow thunder under the piers, and the hundred noises that make the full note of a flood. Once a dripping servant brought him food, but he could not eat; and once he thought that he heard a faint toot from a locomotive across the river, and then he smiled. The bridge's failure would hurt his assistant not a little, hut Hitchcock was a young man with his big work yet to do. For himself the crash meant everything - everything that made a hard life worth the living. They would say, the men of his own profession . . .he remembered the half-pitying things that he himself had said when Lockhart's new waterworks burst and broke down in brick-heaps and sludge, and Lockhart's spirit broke in him and he died. He remembered what he himself had said when the Sumao Bridge went out in the big cyclone by the sea; and most he remembered poor Hartopp's face three weeks later, when the shame had marked it. His bridge was twice the size of Hartopp's, and it carried the Findlayson truss as well as the new pier-shoe - the Findlayson bolted shoe. There were no excuses in his service. Government might listen, perhaps, but his own kind would judge him by his bridge, as that stood or fell. He went over it in his head, plate by plate, span by span, brick by brick, pier by pier, remembering, comparing, estimating, and recalculating, lest there should be any mistake; and through the long hours and through the flights of formulae that danced and wheeled before him a cold fear would come to pinch his heart. His side of the sum was beyond question; but what man knew Mother Gunga's arithmetic? Even as he was making all sure by the multiplication table, the river might be scooping a pot-hole to the very bottom of any one of those eighty-foot piers that carried his reputation. Again a servant came to him with food, but his mouth was dry, and he could only drink and return to the decimals in his brain. And the river was still rising. Peroo, in a mat shelter coat, crouched at his feet, watching now his face and now the face of the river, but saying nothing.

At last the Lascar rose and floundered through the mud towards the village, but he was careful to leave an ally to watch the boats.

Presently he returned, most irreverently driving before him the priest of his creed - a fat old man, with a grey beard that whipped the wind with the wet cloth that blew over his shoulder. Never was seen so lamentable a guru.

"What good are offerings and little kerosene lamps and dry grain," shouted Peroo, "if squatting in the mud is all that thou canst do? Thou hast dealt long with the Gods when they were contented and well-wishing. Now they are angry. Speak to them!"

"What is a man against the wrath of Gods?" whined the priest, cowering as the wind took him. "Let me go to the temple, and I will pray there."

"Son of a pig, pray here! Is there no return for salt fish and curry powder and dried onions? Call aloud! Tell Mother Gunga we have had enough. Bid her be still for the night. I cannot pray, but I have been serving in the Kumpani's boats, and when men did not obey my orders I -" A flourish of the wire-rope colt rounded the sentence, and the priest, breaking free from his disciple, fled to the village.

"Fat pig!" said Peroo. "After all that we have done for him!"

When the flood is down I will see to it that we get a new guru. Finlinson Sahib, it darkens for night now, and since yesterday nothing has been eaten. Be wise, Sahib. No man can endure watching and great thinking on an empty belly. Lie down, Sahib. The river will do what the river will do." "The bridge is mine; I cannot leave it."

"Wilt thou hold it up with thy hands, then?" said Peroo, laughing. "I was troubled for my boats and sheers before the flood came. Now we are in the hands of the

Gods. The Sahib will not eat and lie down? Take these, then. They are meat and good toddy together, and they kill all weariness, besides the fever that follows the rain. I have eaten nothing else to-day at all."

He took a small tin tobacco-box from his sodden waist-belt and thrust it into Findlayson's hand, saying: "Nay, do not be afraid. It is no more than opium - clean Malwa opium."

Findlayson shook two or three of the dark-brown pellets into his hand, and hardly knowing what he did, swallowed them. The stuff was at least a good guard against fever -the fever that was creeping upon him out of the wet mud - and he had seen what Peroo could do in the stewing mists of autumn on the strength of a dose from the tin box.

Peroo nodded with bright eyes. "In a little - in a little the Sahib will find that he thinks well again. I too will -" He dived into his treasure-box, resettled the rain-coat over his head, and squatted down to watch the boats. It was too dark now to see beyond the first pier, and the night seemed to have given the river new strength. Findlayson stood with his chin on his chest, thinking. There was one point about one of the piers - the seventh - that he had not fully settled in his mind. The figures would not shape themselves to the eye except one by one and at enormous intervals of time. There was a sound rich and mellow in his ears like the deepest note of a double-bass - an entrancing sound upon which he pondered for several hours, as it seemed. Then Peroo was at his elbow, shouting that a wire hawser had snapped and the stone-boats were loose. Findlayson saw the fleet open and swing out fanwise to a long-drawn shriek of wire straining across gunnels.

"A tree hit them. They will all go," cried Peroo. "The main hawser has parted. What does the Sahib do?"

An immensely complex plan had suddenly flashed into Findlayson's mind. He saw the ropes running from boat to boat in straight lines and angles - each rope a line of white fire. But there was one rope which was the master rope. He could see that rope. If he could pull it once, it was absolutely and mathematically certain that the disordered fleet would reassemble itself in the backwater behind the guard-tower. But why, he wondered, was Peroo clinging so desperately to his waist as he hastened down the bank? It was necessary to put the Lascar aside, gently and slowly, because it was necessary to save the boats, and, further, to demonstrate the extreme ease of the problem that looked so difficult. And then - but it was of no conceivable importance - a wire-rope raced through his hand, burning it, the high bank disappeared, and with it all the slowly dispersing factors of the problem. He was sitting in the rainy darkness - sitting in a boat that spun like a top, and Peroo was standing over him.

"I had forgotten," said the Lascar, slowly, "that to those fasting and unused, the opium is worse than any wine. Those who die in Gunga go to the Gods. Still, I have no desire to present myself before such great ones. Can the Sahib swim?"

"What need? He can fly - fly as swiftly as the wind," was the thick answer.

"He is mad!" muttered Peroo, under his breath. "And he threw me aside like a bundle of dung-cakes. Well, he will not know his death. The boat cannot live an hour here even if she strike nothing. It is not good to look at death with a clear eye."

He refreshed himself again from the tin box, squatted down in the bows of the reeling, pegged, and stitched craft, staring through the mist at the nothing that was there. A warm drowsiness crept over Findlayson, the Chief Engineer, whose duty was with his bridge. The heavy raindrops struck him with a thousand tingling little thrills, and the weight of all time since time was made hung heavy on his eyelids. He thought and perceived that he was perfectly secure, for the water was so solid that a man could surely step out upon it, and, standing still with his legs apart to keep his balance - this was the most important point - would be borne with great and easy speed to the shore. But yet a better plan came to him. It needed only an exertion of will for the soul to hurl the body ashore as wind drives paper, to waft it kite-fashion to the bank. Thereafter - the boat spun dizzily - suppose the high wind got under the freed body? Would it tower up like a kite and pitch headlong on the far-away sands, or would it duck about, beyond control, through all eternity? Findlayson gripped the gunnel to anchor himself, for it seemed that he was on the edge of taking the flight before he had settled all his plans. Opium has more effect on the white man than the black. Peroo was only comfortably indifferent to accidents. "She cannot live," he grunted. "Her seams open already. If she were even a dinghy with oars we could have ridden it out; but a box with holes is no good. Finlinson Sahib, she fills."

"Accha! I am going away. Come thou also." In his mind, Findlayson had already escaped from the boat, and was circling high in air to find a rest for the sole of his foot. His body - he was really sorry for its gross helplessness - lay in the stern, the water rushing about its knees.

"How very ridiculous!" he said to himself from his eyrie -" that - is Findlayson - chief of the Kashi Bridge. The poor beast is going to be drowned, too. Drowned when it's close to shore. I'm - I'm on shore already. Why doesn't it come along?"

To his intense disgust, he found his soul back in his body again, and that body spluttering and choking in deep water. The pain of the reunion was atrocious, but it was necessary, also, to fight for the body. He was conscious of grasping wildly at wet sand, and striding prodigiously, as one strides in a dream, to keep foothold in the swirling water, till at last he hauled himself clear of the hold of the river, and dropped, panting, on wet earth.

"Not this night," said Peroo, in his ear. "The Gods have protected us." The Lascar moved his feet cautiously, and they rustled among dried stumps. "This is some island of last year's indigo-crop," he went on. "We shall find no men here; but have great care, Sahib; all the snakes of a hundred miles have been flooded out. Here comes the lightning, on the heels of the wind. Now we shall be able to look; but walk carefully."

Findlayson was far and far beyond any fear of snakes, or indeed any merely human emotion. He saw, after he had rubbed the water from his eyes, with an immense clearness, and trod, so it seemed to himself with world-encompassing strides. Somewhere in the night of time he had built a bridge - a bridge that spanned illimitable levels of shining seas; but the Deluge had swept it away, leaving this one island under heaven for Findlayson and his companion, sole survivors of the breed of Man.

An incessant lightning, forked and blue, showed all that there was to be seen on the little patch in the flood - a clump of thorn, a clump of swaying creaking bamboos, and a grey gnarled peepul overshadowing a Hindoo shrine, from whose dome floated a tattered red flag. The holy man whose summer resting-place it was had long since abandoned it, and the weather had broken the red-daubed image of his god. The two men stumbled, heavy-limbed and heavy-eyed, over the ashes of a brick-set cooking-place, and dropped down under the shelter of the branches, while the rain and river roared together.

The stumps of the indigo crackled, and there was a smell of cattle, as a huge and dripping Brahminee bull shouldered his way under the tree. The flashes revealed the trident mark of Shiva on his flank, the insolence of head and hump, the luminous stag-like eyes, the brow crowned with a wreath of sodden marigold blooms, and the silky dewlap that almost swept the ground. There was a noise behind him of other beasts coming up from the flood-line through the thicket, a sound of heavy feet and deep breathing.

"Here be more beside ourselves," said Findlayson, his head against the treepole, looking through half-shut eyes, wholly at ease.

"Truly," said Peroo, thickly, "and no small ones."

"What are they, then? I do not see clearly."

"The Gods. Who else? Look!"

"Ah, true! The Gods surely - the Gods." Findlayson smiled as his head fell forward on his chest. Peroo was eminently right. After the Flood, who should be alive in the land except the Gods that made it - the Gods to whom his village prayed nightly - the Gods who were in all men's mouths and about all men's ways. He could not raise his head or stir a finger for the trance that held him, and Peroo was smiling vacantly at the lightning.

The Bull paused by the shrine, his head lowered to the damp earth. A green Parrot in the branches preened his wet wings and screamed against the thunder as the circle under the tree filled with the shifting shadows of beasts. There was a black Buck at the Bull's heels-such a Buck as Findlayson in his far-away life upon earth might have seen in dreams - a Buck with a royal head, ebon back, silver belly, and gleaming straight horns. Beside him, her head bowed to the ground, the green eyes burning under the heavy brows, with restless tail switching the dead grass, paced a Tigress, full-bellied and deep-jowled.

The Bull crouched beside the shrine, and there leaped from the darkness a monstrous grey Ape, who seated himself man-wise in the place of the fallen image, and the rain spilled like jewels from the hair of his neck and shoulders. Other shadows came and went behind the circle, among them a drunken Man flourishing staff and drinking-bottle. Then a hoarse bellow broke out from near the ground. "The flood lessens even now," it cried. "Hour by hour the water falls, and their bridge still stands!"

"My bridge," said Findlayson to himself "That must be very old work now. What have the Gods to do with my bridge?"

His eyes rolled in the darkness following the roar. A Mugger - the blunt-nosed, ford-haunting Mugger of the Ganges -draggled herself before the beasts, lashing furiously to right and left with her tail.

"They have made it too strong for me. In all this night I have only torn away a handful of planks. The walls stand. The towers stand. They have chained my flood, and the river is not free any more. Heavenly Ones, take this yoke away! Give me clear water between bank and bank! It is I, Mother Gunga, that speak. The Justice of the Gods! Deal me the Justice of the Gods!"

"What said I?" whispered Peroo. "This is in truth a Punchayet of the Gods. Now we know that all the world is dead, save you and I, Sahib."

The Parrot screamed and fluttered again, and the Tigress, her ears flat to her head, snarled wickedly.

Somewhere in the shadow, a great trunk and gleaming tusks swayed to and fro, and a low gurgle broke the silence that followed on the snarl.

"We be here," said a deep voice, "the Great Ones. One only and very many. Shiv, my father, is here, with Indra. Kali has spoken already. Hanuman listens also."

"Kashi is without her Kotwal to-night," shouted the Man with the drinking-bottle, flinging his staff to the ground, while the island rang to the baying of hounds. "Give her the Justice of the Gods."

"Ye were still when they polluted my waters," the great Crocodile bellowed. "Ye made no sign when my river was trapped between the walls. I had no help save my own strength, and that failed - the strength of Mother Gunga failed - before their guard-towers. What could I do? I have done everything. Finish now, Heavenly Ones!"

"I brought the death; I rode the spotted sick-ness from hut to hut of their workmen, and yet they would not cease." A nose-slitten, hide-worn Ass, lame, scissor-legged, and galled, limped forward. "I cast the death at them out of my nostrils, but they would not cease."

Peroo would have moved, but the opium lay heavy upon him.

"Bah!" he said, spitting. "Here is Sitala herself; Mata - the small-pox. Has the Sahib a handkerchief to put over his face?"

"Little help! They fed me the corpses for a month, and I flung them out on my sand-bars, but their work went forward. Demons they are, and sons of demons! And ye left Mother Gunga alone for their fire-carriage to make a mock of The Justice of the Gods on the bridge-builders!"

The Bull turned the cud in his mouth and answered slowly: "If the Justice of the Gods caught all who made a mock of holy things there would be many dark altars in the land, mother."

"But this goes beyond a mock," said the Tigress, darting forward a griping paw. "Thou knowest, Shiv, and ye, too, Heavenly Ones; ye know that they have defiled Gunga. Surely they must come to the Destroyer. Let Indra judge."

The Buck made no movement as he answered: "How long has this evil been?

"Three years, as men count years," said the Mugger, close pressed to the earth.

"Does Mother Gunga die, then, in a year, that she is so anxious to see vengeance now? The deep sea was where she runs but yesterday, and to-morrow the sea shall

cover her again as the Gods count that which men call time. Can any say that this their bridge endures till to-morrow?" said the Buck.

There was a long hush, and in the clearing of the storm the full moon stood up above the dripping trees.

"Judge ye, then," said the River, sullenly. "I have spoken my shame. The flood falls still. I can do no more."

"For my own part " - it was the voice of the great Ape seated within the shrine -" it pleases me well to watch these men, remembering that I also builded no small bridge in the world's youth."

"They say, too," snarled the Tiger, "that these men came of the wreck of thy armies, Hanuman, and therefore thou hast aided -"

"They toil as my armies toiled in Lanka, and they believe that their toil endures. Indra is too high, but Shiv, thou knowest how the land is threaded with their fire-carriages."

"Yea, I know," said the Bull. "Their Gods instructed them in the matter."

A laugh ran round the circle.

"Their Gods! What should their Gods know? They were born yesterday, and those that made them are scarcely yet cold," said the Mugger. "To-morrow their Gods will die."

"Ho!" said Peroo. "Mother Gunga talks good talk. I told that to the padre-sahib who preached on the Mombassa, and he asked the Burra Malum to put me in irons for a great rudeness."

"Surely they make these things to please their Gods," said the Bull again.

"Not altogether," the Elephant rolled forth. "It is for the profit of my mahajuns - my fat money-lenders that worship me at each new year, when they draw my image at the head of the account-books. I, looking over their shoulders by lamplight, see that the names in the books are those of men in far places - for all the towns are drawn together by the fire-carriage, and the money comes and goes swiftly, and the account-books grow as fat as - myself. And I, who am Ganesh of Good Luck, I bless my peoples."

"They have changed the face of the land-which is my land. They have killed and made new towns on my banks," said the Mugger.

"It is but the shifting of a little dirt. Let the dirt dig in the dirt if it pleases the dirt," answered the Elephant.

"But afterwards?" said the Tiger. "Afterwards they will see that Mother Gunga can avenge no insult, and they fall away from her first, and later from us all, one by one. In the end, Ganesh, we are left with naked altars."

The drunken Man staggered to his feet, and hiccupped vehemently.

"Kali lies. My sister lies. Also this my stick is the Kotwal of Kashi, and he keeps tally of my pilgrims. When the time comes to worship Bhairon-and it is always time - the fire-carriages move one by one, and each bears a thousand pilgrims. They do not come afoot any more, but rolling upon wheels, and my honour is increased."

"Gunga, I have seen thy bed at Pryag black with the pilgrims," said the Ape, leaning forward, "and but for the fire-carriage they would have come slowly and in fewer numbers. Remember."

"They come to me always," Bhairon went on thickly. "By day and night they pray to me, all the Common People in the fields and the roads. Who is like Bhairon to-day? What talk is this of changing faiths? Is my staff Kotwal of Kashi for nothing?

He keeps the tally, and he says that never were so many altars as today, and the firecarriage serves them well. Bhairon am I - Bhairon of the Common People, and the chiefest of the Heavenly Ones to-day. Also my staff says -"

"Peace, thou" lowed the Bull. "The worship of the schools is mine, and they talk very wisely, asking whether I be one or many, as is the delight of my people, and ye know what I am. Kali, my wife, thou knowest also."

"Yea, I know," said the Tigress, with lowered head.

"Greater am I than Gunga also. For ye know who moved the minds of men that they should count Gunga holy among the rivers. Who die in that water - ye know how men say - come to us without punishment, and Gunga knows that the fire-carriage has borne to her scores upon scores of such anxious ones; and Kali knows that she has held her chiefest festivals among the pilgrimages that are fed by the fire-carriage. Who smote at Pooree, under the Image there, her thousands in a day and a night, and bound the sickness to the wheels of the fire-carriages, so that it ran from one end of the land to the other? Who but Kali? Before the fire-carriage came it was a heavy toil. The fire-carriages have served thee well, Mother of Death. But I speak for mine own altars, who am not Bhairon of the Common Folk, but Shiv. Men go to and fro, making words and telling talk of strange Gods, and I listen. Faith follows faith among my people in the schools, and I have no anger; for when all words are said, and the new talk is ended, to Shiv men return at the last."

"True. It is true," murmured Hanuman. "To Shiv and to the others, mother, they return. I creep from temple to temple in the North, where they worship one God and His Prophet; and presently my image is alone within their shrines."

"Small thanks," said the Buck, turning his head slowly. "I am that One and His Prophet also."

"Even so, father," said Hanuman. "And to the South I go who am the oldest of the Gods as men know the Gods, and presently I touch the shrines of the New Faith and the Woman whom we know is hewn twelve-armed, and still they call her Mary."

"Small thanks, brother," said the Tigress. "I am that Woman."

"Even so, sister; and I go West among the fire-carriages, and stand before the bridge-builders in many shapes, and because of me they change their faiths and are very wise. Ho! ho! I am the builder of bridges, indeed - bridges between this and that, and each bridge leads surely to Us in the end. Be content, Gunga. Neither these men nor those that follow them mock thee at all."

"Am I alone, then, Heavenly Ones? Shall I smooth out my flood lest unhappily I bear away their walls? Will Indra dry my springs in the hills and make me crawl humbly between their wharfs? Shall I bury me in the sand ere I offend?"

"And all for the sake of a little iron bar with the fire-carriage atop. Truly, Mother Gunga is always young!" said Ganesh the Elephant. "A child had not spoken more foolishly. Let the dirt dig in the dirt ere it return to the dirt. I know only that my people grow rich and praise me. Shiv has said that the men of the schools do not forget; Bhairon is content for his crowd of the Common People; and Hanuman laughs."

"Surely I laugh," said the Ape. "My altars are few beside those of Ganesh or Bhairon, but the fire-carriages bring me new worshippers from beyond the Black Water - the men who believe that their God is toil. I run before them beckoning, and they follow Hanuman."

"Give them the toil that they desire, then," said the River.

"Make a bar across my flood and throw the water back upon the bridge. Once thou wast strong in Lanka, Hanuman. Stoop and lift my bed."

"Who gives life can take life." The Ape scratched in the mud with a long forefinger.

"And yet, who would profit by the killing? Very many would die."

There came up from the water a snatch of a love-song such as the boys sing when they watch their cattle in the noon heats of late spring. The Parrot screamed joyously, sidling along his branch with lowered head as the song grew louder, and in a patch of clear moonlight stood revealed the young herd, the darling of the Gopis, the idol of dreaming maids and of mothers ere their children are born Krishna the Well-beloved. He stooped to knot up his long wet hair, and the Parrot fluttered to his shoulder.

"Fleeting and singing, and singing and fleeting," hiccupped Bhairon. "Those make thee late for the council, brother."

"And then?" said Krishna, with a laugh, throwing back his head. "Ye can do little without me or Karma here." He fondled the Parrot's plumage and laughed again. "What is this sitting and talking together? I heard Mother Gunga roaring in the dark, and so came quickly from a hut where I lay warm. And what have ye done to Karma, that he is so wet and silent? And what does Mother Gunga here? Are the heavens full that ye must come paddling in the mud beast-wise? Karma, what do they do?"

"Gunga has prayed for a vengeance on the bridge-builders, and Kali is with her. Now she bids Hanuman whelm the bridge, that her honour may be made great," cried the Parrot. "I waited here, knowing that thou wouldst come, O my master!

"And the Heavenly Ones said nothing? Did Gunga and the Mother of Sorrows out-talk them? Did none speak for my people?"

"Nay," said Ganesh, moving uneasily from foot to foot; "I said it was but dirt at play, and why should we stamp it flat?"

"I was content to let them toil -well content," said Hanuman.

"What had I to do with Gunga's anger?" said the Bull.

"I am Bhairon of the Common Folk, and this my staff is Kotwal of all Kashi. I spoke for the Common People."

"Thou?" The young God's eyes sparkled.

"Am I not the first of the Gods in their mouths to-day?" returned Bhairon, unabashed. "For the sake of the Common People I said - very many wise things which I have now forgotten, but this my staff-"

Krishna turned impatiently, saw the Mugger at his feet, and kneeling, slipped an arm round the cold neck. "Mother," he said gently, "get thee to thy flood again. The matter is not for thee. What harm shall thy honour take of this live dirt? Thou hast given them their fields new year after year, and by thy flood they are made strong. They come all to thee at the last. What need to slay them now? Have pity, mother, for a little - and it is only for a little."

"If it be only for a little," the slow beast began.

"Are they Gods, then?" Krishna returned with a laugh, his eyes looking into the dull eyes of the River. "Be certain that it is only for a little. The Heavenly Ones have heard thee, and presently justice will be done. Go now, mother, to the flood again. Men and cattle are thick on the waters - the banks fall - the villages melt because of thee."

"But the bridge - the bridge stands." The Mugger turned grunting into the undergrowth as Krishna rose.

"It is ended," said the Tigress, viciously. "There is no more justice from the Heavenly Ones. Ye have made shame and sport of Gunga, who asked no more than a few score lives."

"Of my people - who lie under the leaf-roofs of the village yonder - of the young girls, and the young men who sing to them in the dark -of the child that will be born next morn - of that which was begotten to-night," said Krishna. "And when all is done, what profit? To-morrow sees them at work. Ay, if ye swept the bridge out from end to end they would begin anew. Hear me! Bhairon is drunk always. Hanuman mocks his people with new riddles."

"Nay, but they are very old ones," the Ape said, laughing.

"Shiv hears the talk of the schools and the dreams of the holy men; Ganesh thinks only of his fat traders; but I - I live with these my people, asking for no gifts, and so receiving them hourly."

"And very tender art thou of thy people," said the Tigress.

"They are my own. The old women dream of me turning in their sleep; the maids look and listen for me when they go to fill their lotahs by the river. I walk by the young men waiting without the gates at dusk, and I call over my shoulder to the white-beards. Ye know, Heavenly Ones, that I alone of us all walk upon the earth continually, and have no pleasure in our heavens so long as a green blade springs here, or there are two voices at twilight in the standing crops. Wise are ye, but ye live far off; forgetting whence ye came. So do I not forget. And the fire-carriage feeds your shrines, ye say? And the fire-carriages bring a thousand pilgrims where but ten came in the old years? True. That is true, to-day."

"But to-morrow they are dead, brother," said Ganesh.

"Peace!" said the Bull, as Hanuman leaned forward again. "And to-morrow, beloved - what of to-morrow?"

"This only. A new word creeping from mouth to mouth among the Common Folk - a word that neither man nor God can lay hold of - an evil word - a little lazy word among the Common Folk, saying (and none know who set that word afoot) that they weary of ye, Heavenly Ones."

The Gods laughed together softly. "And then, beloved," they said.

"And to cover that weariness they, my people, will bring to thee, Shiv, and to thee, Ganesh, at first greater offerings and a louder noise of worship. But the word has gone abroad, and, after, they will pay fewer dues to your fat Brahmins. Next they will forget your altars, but so slowly that no man can say how his forgetfulness began."

"I knew - I knew! I spoke this also, but they would not hear," said the Tigress. "We should have slain-we should have slain!"

"It is too late now. Ye should have slain at the beginning when the men from across the water had taught our folk nothing. Now my people see their work, and go away thinking. They do not think of the Heavenly Ones altogether. They think of the fire-carriage and the other things that the bridge-builders have done, and when your priests thrust forward hands asking alms, they give a little unwillingly. That is the beginning, among one or two, or five or ten - for I, moving among my people, know what is in their hearts."

"And the end, Jester of the Gods? What shall the end be?" said Ganesh.

"The end shall be as it was in the beginning, O slothful son of Shiv! The flame shall die upon the altars and the prayer upon the tongue till ye become little Gods again - Gods of the jungle - names that the hunters of rats and noosers of dogs whisper in the thicket and among the caves -rag-Gods, pot Godlings of the tree, and the village-mark, as ye were at the beginning. That is the end, Ganesh, for thee, and for Bhairon - Bhairon of the Common People."

"It is very far away," grunted Bhairon. "Also, it is a lie."

"Many women have kissed Krishna. They told him this to cheer their own hearts when the grey hairs came, and he has told us the tale," said the Bull, below his breath.

"Their Gods came, and we changed them. I took the Woman and made her twelve-armed. So shall we twist all their Gods," said Hanuman.

"Their Gods! This is no question of their Gods - one or three - man or woman. The matter is with the people. I move, and not the Gods of the bridge-builders," said Krishna.

"So be it. I have made a man worship the fire-carriage as it stood still breathing smoke, and he knew not that he worshipped me," said Hanuman the Ape. "They will only change a little the names of their Gods. I shall lead the builders of the bridges as of old; Shiv shall be worshipped in the schools by such as doubt and despise their fellows; Ganesh shall have his mahajuns, and Bhairon the donkey-drivers, the pilgrims, and the sellers of toys. Beloved, they will do no more than change the names, and that we have seen a thousand times."

"Surely they will do no more than change the names," echoed Ganesh; but there was an uneasy movement among the Gods.

"They will change more than the names. Me alone they cannot kill, so long as a maiden and a man meet together or the spring follows the winter rains. Heavenly Ones, not for nothing have I walked upon the earth. My people know not now what they know; but I, who live with them, I read their hearts. Great Kings, the beginning of the end is born already. The fire-carriages shout the names of new Gods that are not the old under new names. Drink now and eat greatly! Bathe your faces in the smoke of the altars before they grow cold! Take dues and listen to the cymbals and the drums, Heavenly Ones, while yet there are flowers and songs. As men count time the end is far off; but as we who know reckon it is to-day. I have spoken."

The young God ceased, and his brethren looked at each other long in silence.

"This I have not heard before," Peroo whispered in his companion's ear. "And yet sometimes, when I oiled the brasses in the engine-room of the Goorkha, I have wondered if our priests were so wise - so wise. The day is coming, Sahib. They will be gone by the morning."

A yellow light broadened in the sky, and the tone of the river changed as the darkness withdrew.

Suddenly the Elephant trumpeted aloud as though man had goaded him.

"Let Indra judge. Father of all, speak thou! What of the things

we have heard? Has Krishna lied indeed? Or—"

"Ye know," said the Buck, rising to his feet. "Ye know the Riddle of the Gods. When Brahm ceases to dream, the Heavens and the Hells and Earth disappear. Be content. Brahm dreams still. The dreams come and go, and the nature of the dreams changes, but still Brahm dreams. Krishna has walked too long upon earth, and yet I love him the more for the tale he has told. The Gods change, beloved - all save One!"

"Ay, all save one that makes love in the hearts of men," said Krishna, knotting his girdle. "It is but a little time to wait, and ye shall know if I lie. Truly it is but a little time, as thou sayest, and we shall know. Get thee to thy huts again, beloved, and make sport for the young things, for still Brahm dreams. Go, my children! Brahm dreams and till he wakes the Gods die not."

"Whither went they?" said the Lascar, awe-struck, shivering a little with the cold.

"God knows!" said Findlayson. The river and the island lay in full daylight now, and there was never mark of hoof or pug on the wet earth under the peepul. Only a parrot screamed in the branches, bringing down showers of water-drops as he fluttered his wings.

"Up! We are cramped with cold! Has the opium died out. Canst thou move, Sahib?"

Findlayson staggered to his feet and shook himself. His bead swam and ached, but the work of the opium was over, and, as he sluiced his forehead in a pool, the Chief Engineer of the Kashi Bridge was wondering how he had managed to fall upon the island, what chances the day offered of return, and, above all, how his work stood.

"Peroo, I have forgotten much I was under the guard-tower watching the river; and then --- Did the flood sweep us away?"

"No. The boats broke loose, Sahib, and" (if the Sahib had forgotten about the opium, decidedly Peroo would not remind him) "in striving to retie them, so it seemed to me but it was dark - a rope caught the Sahib and threw him upon a boat. Considering that we two, with Hitchcock Sahib, built, as it were, that bridge, I came also upon the boat, which came riding on horseback, as it were, on the nose of this island, and so, splitting, cast us ashore. I made a great cry when the boat left the wharf and without doubt Hitchcock Sahib will come for us. As for the bridge, so many have died in the building that it cannot fall." A fierce sun, that drew out all the smell of the sodden land, had followed the storm, and in that clear light there was no room for a man to think of the dreams of the dark. Findlayson stared upstream, across the blaze of moving water, till his eyes ached. There was no sign of any bank to the Ganges, much less of a bridge-line.

"We came down far," he said. "It was wonderful that we were not drowned a hundred times."

"That was the least of the wonder, for no man dies before his time. I have seen Sydney, I have seen London, and twenty great ports, but" - Peroo looked at the damp, discoloured shrine under the peepul - "never man has seen that we saw here."

"What?"

"Has the Sahib forgotten; or do we black men only see the Gods?"

"There was a fever upon me." Findlayson was still looking uneasily across the water. "It seemed that the island was full of beasts and men talking, but I do not remember. A boat could live in this water now, I think."

"Oho! Then it is true. 'When Brahm ceases to dream, the Gods die.' Now I know, indeed, what he meant. Once, too, the guru said as much to me; but then I did not understand. Now I am wise."

"What?" said Findlayson, over his shoulder.

Peroo went on as if he were talking to himself "Six - seven - ten monsoons since, I was watch on the fo'c'sle of the Rewah - the Kumpani's big boat - and there was a big tufan; green and black water beating, and I held fast to the life-lines, choking under the waters. Then I thought of the Gods - of Those whom we saw to-night "-

he stared curiously at Findlayson's back, but the white man was looking across the flood. "Yes, I say of Those whom we saw this night past, and I called upon Them to protect me. And while I prayed, still keeping my lookout, a big wave came and threw me forward upon the ring of the great black bow-anchor, and the Rewah rose high and high, leaning towards the left-hand side, and the water drew away from beneath her nose, and I lay upon my belly, holding the ring, and looking down into those great deeps. Then I thought, even in the face of death: If I lose hold I die, and for me neither the Rewah nor my place by the galley where the rice is cooked, nor Bombay, nor Calcutta, nor even London, will be any more for me. 'How shall I be sure,' I said, 'that the Gods to whom I pray will abide at all?' This I thought, and the Rewah dropped her nose as a hammer falls, and all the sea came in and slid me backwards along the fo'c'sle and over the break of the fo'c'sle, and I very badly bruised my shin against the donkey-engine: but I did not die, and I have seen the Gods. They are good for live men, but for the dead.... They have spoken Themselves. Therefore, when I come to the village I will beat the guru for talking riddles which are no riddles. When Brahm ceases to dream the Gods go."

"Look up-stream. The light blinds. Is there smoke yonder?"

Peroo shaded his eyes with his hands. "He is a wise man and quick. Hitchcock Sahib would not trust a rowboat. He has borrowed the Rao Sahib's steam-launch, and comes to look for us. I have always said that there should have been a steam-launch on the bridge works for us.

The territory of the Rao of Baraon lay within ten miles of the bridge; and Findlayson and Hitchcock had spent a fair portion of their scanty leisure in playing billiards and shooting blackbuck with the young man. He had been bearled by an English tutor of sporting tastes for some five or six years, and was now royally wasting the revenues accumulated during his minority by the Indian Government. His steam-launch, with its silver-plated rails, striped silk awning, and mahogany decks, was a new toy which Findlayson had found horribly in the way when the Rao came to look at the bridge works.

"It's great luck," murmured Findlayson, but he was none the less afraid, wondering what news might be of the bridge.

The gaudy blue-and-white funnel came downstream swiftly. They could see Hitchcock in the bows, with a pair of opera-glasses, and his face was unusually white. Then Peroo hailed, and the launch made for the tail of the island. The Rao Sahib, in tweed shooting-suit and a seven-hued turban, waved his royal hand, and Hitchcock shouted. But he need have asked no questions, for Findlayson's first demand was for his bridge.

"All serene! 'Gad, I never expected to see you again, Findlayson. You're seven koss downstream. Yes; there's not a stone shifted anywhere; but how are you? I borrowed the Rao Sahib's launch, and he was good enough to come along. Jump in. "Ah, Finlinson, you are very well, eh? That was most unprecedented calamity last night, eh? My royal palace, too, it leaks like the devil, and the crops will also be short all about my country. Now you shall back her out, Hitchcock. I - I do not understand steam-engines. You are wet? You are cold, Finlinson? I have some things to eat here, and you will take a good drink."

"I'm immensely grateful, Rao Sahib. I believe you've saved my life. How did Hitchcock -"

"Oho! His hair was upon end. He rode to me in the middle of the night and woke me up in the arms of Morpheus. I was most truly concerned, Finlinson, so I came too. My head-priest he is very angry just now. We will go quick, Mister Hitchcock. I am due to attend at twelve forty-five in the state temple, where we sanctify some new idol. If not so I would have asked you to spend the day with me. They are dam-bore, these religious ceremonies, Finlinson, eh?"

Peroo, well known to the crew, had possessed himself of the inlaid wheel, and was taking the launch craftily up-stream. But while he steered he was, in his mind, handling two feet of partially untwisted wire-rope; and the back upon which he beat was the back of his guru.

Rudyard Kipling – A Biography

Born in Bombay on 30th December 1865, Joseph Rudyard Kipling wrote short stories, poems and novels, a body of work whose reputation is in constant flux as his presentations and interpretations of empire are viewed within the changing context of empirical absolution in the twentieth century. Having spent the first five years of his life in India he felt a natural affinity for the country, though his upbringing had a distinctly colonial taste flavour. He was born in the Bombay Presidency of British India to Lockwood Kipling, an English art teacher and illustrator who took a position as professor of architectural sculpture in the Jeejeebhoy School of Art and Alice MacDonald, spoken of by the a Viceroy of India that "dullness and Mrs Kipling cannot exist in the same room". Though their presence in India was principally artistic and educational, rather than political, the company they kept and the establishments in which they they kept it indicate an existence very much benefitting from the British Empire. Lockwood would later go on to assume a position as curator of the Lahore Museum, while working on various illustrations for Rudyard's writing, and various decorations for the Victoria and Albert museum in London. Much of his work, then, was coloured by the empire, whether in service to or benefitting from, and it was into this distinctly British experience of India that Rudyard was born.

Lockwood and Alice had met and fallen in love at Rudyard Lake in Rudyard, Staffordshire, and their affections for the area were so great they chose to refer to the lake in naming their first-born. Alice came from a family of four sisters, all of whose marriages were significant and well-arranged; moreover, Rudyard's most famous relative was Stanley Baldwin, Conservative Prime Minister on three occasions in the 1920s and 1930s. Kipling's sense of belonging in Bombay is found in 'To the City of Bombay' in the dedication to Seven Seas, a collection of poems published in 1900, which reads
> Mother of Cities to me,
> For I was born in her gate,

Between the palms and the sea,
Where the world-end steamers wait.

His parents considered themselves Anglo-Indians, and he would later assume this classification although he did not live there long. His first five years, which he describes as days of "strong light and darkness", ended when he and his three-year-old sister Alice were removed to Southsea, Plymouth, to board with Captain Pryse Agar Holloway and his wife Mrs Sarah Holloway, a couple who cared for the children of couples born in British India. They were there for six years and Kipling would later recall their time there with horror, describing incidents of cruelty and neglect and wondering whether it was these which speeded up his literary maturity, for "it made me give attention to the lies I soon found it necessary to tell: and this, I presume, is the foundation of literary effort".

Alice's time, by contrast, was relatively comfortable, Mrs Holloway hoping that she would marry her son, though this ambition would not come to fruition. They did have relatives in England, a maternal aunt Georgiana and her husband who lived in Fulham, London, in a house at which they spent a month each Christmas and which Kipling later described as "a paradise which I verily believe saved me". Their mother returned in 1877 and removed them from their custody with the Holloways. A year later he gained admission to the United Services College at Westward Ho! in Devon, a recently established school with the intention of readying boys for military service in the British Army. His time here was fraught physically, though emotionally it proved fruitful for he began several firm friendships with other boys at the school. Moreover, he found in it inspiration for the setting of his series of schoolboy stories, Stalky and Co, begun in 1899. Meanwhile, his sister Alice had returned to Southsea and was boarding with Florence Garrard, with whom he fell in love and on whom he modeled Maisie in his first novel, The Light That Failed, published in 1891. At sixteen he was found lacking in the academic perspicacity necessary to undertake a scholarship to Oxford University, his parents meanwhile lacking the wherewithal to finance him therein. As such his father sought a job for him in Lahore, Punjab, where he was now a museum curator. The position he found for his son was as assistant editor of the Civil and Military Gazette, a small local newspaper. Kipling left for India on 20th September 1882, arriving in Bombay on 18th October. "There were yet three or four days" rail to Lahore, where my people lived. After these, my English years fell away, nor ever, I think, came back in full strength".

The Gazette appeared six days of the week, year-round save for a short break at both Christmas and Easter. Its editor Stephen Wheeler was diligent but Kipling's writing was insatiable, and he came to consider the paper his "mistress and most true love". In the summer of 1883 Kipling visited Shimla, the colonial hill-station and summer capital of British India which was then called Simla. Chosen by the British owing to its resemblance of English climate and scenery (as far as was possible in India), it became the seat of the Viceroy of India for the six months on the plains which were too hot for the British temperament, and subsequently became a "centre of power as well as pleasure". Lockwood was asked to serve in the Church there, and his family became yearly visitors while Kipling himself would take his annual leave here from 1885-88. The value of this time is evident from the regularity with which Simla appears in his writing for the Gazette, which in his journals he describes the time as

> "pure joy - every golden hour counted. It began in heat and discomfort, by rail and road. It ended in the cool evening, with a wood fire in one's bedroom, and next morn - thirty more of them ahead! - the early cup of tea, the Mother who brought it in, and the long talks of us all together again."

In 1886, his Departmental Ditties appeared, his first collection of verse, and brought with it a change of editor; Kay Robinson, Wheeler's replacement, was in favour of Kipling's creativity and granted him more freedom in that respect, even asking him to write short stories to appear in the newspaper. The vivacity of his writing was captured in a description of him by an ex-colleague at the Gazette, saying he "never knew such a fellow for ink - he simply revelled in it, filling up his pen viciously, and then throwing the contents all over the office, so that it was almost dangerous to approach him". While in Lahore, he had thirty-nine stories published in the Gazette between November 1886 and June 1887. Most of these are compiled in Plain Tales from the Hills, his first collection of prose, which was published in January 1888 in Calcutta, shortly after his 22nd birthday. In November 1887, he transferred from the Gazette to its much larger sister newspaper, The Pioneer, based in Allahabad. The pace of his writing remained, and in 1888 he published six collections of stories, Soldiers Three, The Story of the Gadsbys, In Black and White, Under the Deodars, The Phantom Rickshaw and Wee Willie Winkie, composed of some 41 stories. In addition, his position as The Pioneer's special correspondent in the Western region of Rajputna, he wrote many sketches which were plater compiled in Letters of Marque and published in From Sea to Sea and OTher Sketches, Letters of Travel.

A dispute in 1889 saw him discharged from The Pioneer, though by now he had been considering his future and sold the rights to his six volumes of stories for £200 and a small royalty, while the Plain Tales fetched £50, along with six months' salary from The Pioneer in lieu of notice. Using the money to undertake a pilgrimage to London, the literary centre of the British Empire, he left India on 9th March 1889, travelling via Rangoon, San Francisco, Hong Kong and Japan, then through the United States writing articles for The Pioneer which were also included in From Sea to Sea and Other Sketches, Letters of Travel. Arriving in England at Liverpool on October 1889, London and his literary début there beckoned.

His first task was to find a place to live, and he eventually settled on quarters in Villiers Street, Strand. The next two years saw several stories accepted by various magazine editors, the publication of the novel The Light That Failed, a nervous breakdown, the collaboration with Wolcott Balestier on the novel (uncharacterstically misspelt) The Naulhaka, and in 1891, following his doctors' advice, he embarked on a further sea voyage, travelling to South Africa, Australia, New Zealand and also returning to India. His plans to spend Christmas with his family were cut short on the news of Balestier's sudden death from typhoid fever, prompting an immediate return to London. Before he left, he had proposed to Balestier's sister Caroline Starr Balestier, with whom he had been having a hushed romance for just over a year. Back in London, Life's Handicap was published in 1891, a collection of short stories whose subject was the British in India, and British India. On 18th January 1892 aged 26 he married Caroline in the midst of an epidemic of influenza. Caroline was given away by Henry James, the famous and celebrated American author.

Honeymooning in Japan, they travelled via Vermont, America, to visit the Balestier estate, and upon arrival in Yokahama they found that their bank, The New Oriental Banking Corporation, had failed, though this loss did not deter them and they returned to Vermont, Caroline now pregnant with their first child. Renting a cottage on a farm for $10 per month, they lived a spartan existence and were "extraordinarily and self-centredly content". The named the residence Bliss Cottage, and it was here that the child was born, named Josephine, "in three foot of snow on the night of 29th December 1892. Her Mother's birthday being the 31st and mine the 30th we congratulated her on her sense of the fitness of things." While here, Kipling had his first ideas for the Jungle Books. Shortly after Josephine was born the couple moved in pursuit of more space and comfort, buying ten acres overlooking the Connecticut River from Caroline's brother. The house they built there was inspired by the Mughul architecture he encountered in Lahore, and was named Naulakha (this time correctly spelt) in honour of Wolcott. His literary output in four years here included the Jungle Books, a collection of short stories entitled The Day's Work, the novel Captain Courageous and a plethora of poetry, of which most notably the volume The Seven Seas and his Barrack-Room Ballads. Meanwhile, he enjoyed correspondence with the many children who wrote to him about the Jungle Books.

In between this writing, Kipling took regular visitors. Most notably Arthur Conan Doyle came, bringing golf clubs and staying for two days to give Kipling an extended golf lesson. Kipling enjoyed the game so much that he continued to play, even in winter with special red balls, though he found that the ice would lead to drives travelling two miles as they slid "down the long slope to the Connecticut River". Elsie, the couple's second daughter, was born in February 1896, and by this time it is thought that their marriage had lost its original spark of spontaneity and descended into routine, though they remained loyal to one another. By now, failed arbitration between the United States and England over a border dispute involving British Guiana incited Anglo-American tensions which, in May 1896, resulted in a confrontation between Kipling and Caroline's brother, resulting in his arrest and, in the hearing which followed, the destruction of Kipling's private life, leaving him exhausted and miserable and leading to their return to England.

They had settled Torquay, Devon, by September 1896, and he remained socially present and literarily productive. The success of his writing had brought him fame, and he had responded with a sense of duty to include in his writing elements of political persuasion, most notably in his two poems Recessional and The White Man's Burden, which caused controversy when they were published in 1897 and 1899 respectively. Many considered them anthemic to the empire, propaganda for the imperial mindset so prevalent in the Victoria era. Their first son, John, was born in August 1887. Another journey to South Africa began a tradition of wintering there, which continued until 1908. His reputation as Poet of the Empire saw him well-received by politicians in the Cape Colony, and he started the newspaper The Friend for Lord Roberts and the British troops in Bloemfontein. Back in England, they moved to Rottingdean, East Sussex, in 1897, and in 1902 he bought Bateman's, a house built in 1630, which was his home from until his death in 1936. Kim was published in 1902, after which he collected material for Just So Stories for Little Children, published a year later. Both he and Josephine developed pneumonia while visiting the United States, from which she later died.

This decade proved his most successful, being awarded the Nobel Prize for Literature in 1907, the prize citation reading "in consideration of the power of observation, originality of imagination, virility of ideas and remarkable talent for narration which characterise the creations of this world-famous author". He was the first English-language recipient. At the award ceremony in Switzerland, Carl David af Wirsén praised Kipling and the English literary tradition:

> The Swedish Academy, in awarding the Nobel Prize in Literature this year to Rudyard Kipling, desires to pay a tribute to the literature of England, so rich in manifold glories, and to the greatest genius in the realm of narrative that that country has produced in our times.

Following this achievement, Kipling published Rewards and Fairies, which contained If, voted Britain's favourite poem in a BBC opinion poll in 1995. He turned down several recommendations for knighthood and was considered for Poet Laureate, though this position was never offered to him.

The sense of perseverance, honour and stoicism in If prevailed in many of his opinions, including that on the First World War. Writing in The New Army in Training in 1915, he scorned those who refused conscription, considering

> what will be the position in years to come of the young man who has deliberately elected to outcaste himself from this all-embracing brotherhood? What of his family, and, above all, what of his descendants, when the books have been closed and the last balance struck of sacrifice and sorrow in every hamlet, village, parish, suburb, city, shire, district, province, and Dominion throughout the Empire?

This attitude saw him encourage his son, John, to go to war, and he was promptly killed at the Battle of Loos in September 1915, aged 18. Last seen during the battle stumbling blindly through the mud, screaming in agony after an exploding shell had ripped his face apart, Kipling would write "If any question why we died / Tell them, because our fathers lied", perhaps betraying the guilt he felt at encouraging his son to go to war and finding him a position in the Irish Guards through his friendship with commander-in-chief Lord Roberts, for whom he had established The Friend in Bloemfontein. His death inspired much of Kipling's successive writing, notably My Boy Jack and a two-volume history of the Irish Guards, considered one of the finest examples of regimental history. Ironically, though his writing and his political position had arguably cost John his life, after the war he became friends with a French soldier whose copy of Kim, kept in his breast pocket, had stopped a bullet and saved his life. For a while the book and the soldier's Croix de Guerre were with Kipling, presented as tokens of gratitude, and they remained in contact, though when Kipling learned of the soldier's child he insisted on returning both book and medal.

He kept writing until 1930, though at a considerably slower pace, and to less success. His death, already once incorrectly announced early by a magazine in a premature obituary (and to which he responded "I've just read that I am dead. Don't forget to delete me from your list of subscribers") came on 18th January 1936, at the age of 70, from a perforated duodenal ulcer. His coffin was carried by, among others, his cousin the Prime Minister Stanley Baldwin, and his marble casket covered by a Union flag. He was cremated at Golders Green Crematorium in Northwest London and his ashes are buried at Poets' Corner in Westminster Abbey, alongside the graves of both Charles Dickens and Thomas Hardy. In conjunction with various earthly memorials which commemorate him, alongside his extensive writing, he has a crater on Mercury named after him. The question of memorial and monument is much-addressed in English Literature and, as various great authors and poets have agreed before Kipling's time, his memory lives on more vivaciously set in his words, far longer and better represented than it could set in stone.

www.ingramcontent.com/pod-product-compliance
Lightning Source LLC
Chambersburg PA
CBHW070812120626
46557CB00002B/828